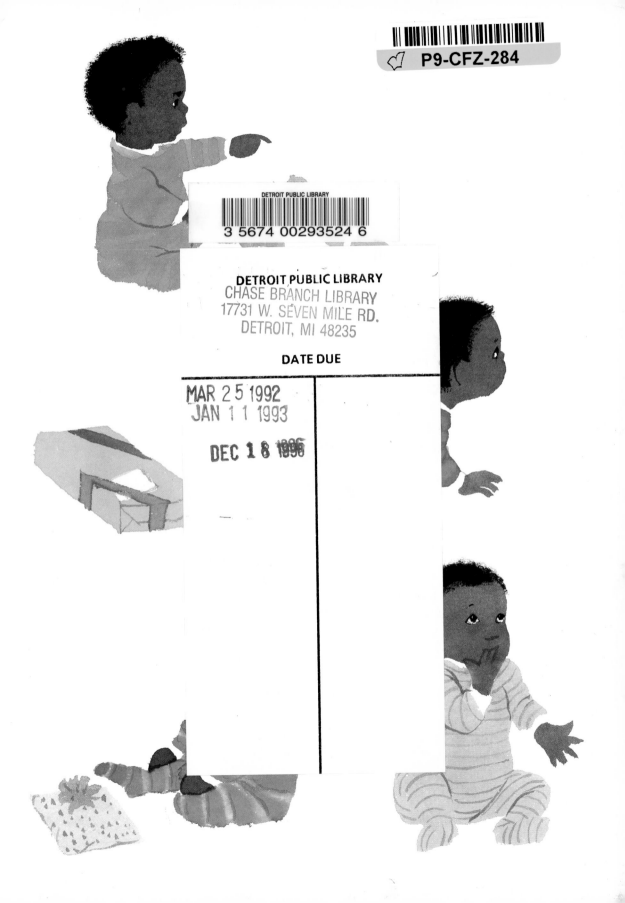

For Morcea and her family

Text copyright ©1986 by Sarah Hayes.
Illustrations copyright © 1986 by
Jan Ormerod.
First published in Great Britain by
Walker Books Ltd. in 1986.

Printed in Italy.
First U.S. Edition 1986.   1   2   3   4   5   6   7   8   9   10

**Library of Congress Cataloging in Publication Data**
Hayes, Sarah.
  Happy Christmas, Gemma.
  Summary: Little Gemma and her family prepare for
Christmas all week and have a happy celebration on
the day.
  [1. Christmas—Fiction.   2. Afro-Americans—
Fiction]   I. Ormerod, Jan, ill.   II. Title.
PZ7.H314873Hap    1986    [E]    85-23674
ISBN 0-688-06508-2

# HAPPY
# CHRISTMAS
# GEMMA

Written by
## Sarah Hayes

Illustrated by
## Jan Ormerod

Lothrop, Lee & Shepard Books
New York

First of all we made
the Christmas pudding.
I stirred the mixture
and made a wish.
Gemma threw the spoon
on the floor.

Another day
we put up the decorations.
I made a long paper chain.
Gemma made a mess.

A week before Christmas
we decorated the tree.
I was big enough to
put the angel on the top.
Gemma pulled off a star.

Then we wrapped our presents.
I cut the sticky tape.
Gemma tore up some labels.

On Christmas Eve
we hung up the stockings.
I had a big red stocking.
Gemma had a little red sock.
Then we went to bed.
I stayed awake
and listened for
Santa Claus.
Gemma went to sleep.

Then it was Christmas Day.
I had lots of little things
in my stocking.
Gemma had some chocolate money
and two cows,
which she said were two dogs.

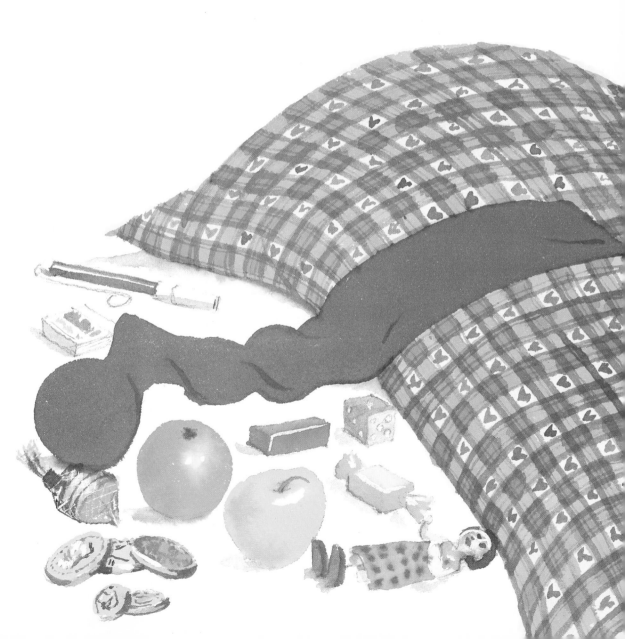

On Christmas morning
Grandma took us all to church.
Then we opened our presents
and telephoned our friends
and relations.
I talked to my cousin
in Jamaica.
Gemma talked to someone too.

We all ate a lot at Christmas dinner.
Once Grandma put her elbows
on the table, but I didn't say anything.
Gemma turned her bowl
upside down.

Then Gemma disappeared.
I hunted and hunted.
Gemma wasn't anywhere around.

I looked in the cupboard.
Gemma was in there,
eating the icing
off Grandma's Christmas cake.

After supper Gemma was tired.
I wasn't.
I said,
"Happy Christmas, Gemma."
Gemma said, "Dog."

Then we sang carols.
I sang one on my own.
Gemma didn't sing any.
She was fast asleep.